# Navya Sings for Navarathri

**HARPER**
*An Imprint of HarperCollinsPublishers*

## AUTHOR'S NOTE

*T*he celebrations in this story are based on recollections of my childhood. Navarathri was one of my favorite festivals. It got us more than a week off from school!

Before every Navarathri, my brother would crawl up the loft space to pull out the crate of dolls. As a women-only festival, the role of men was limited to helping with the arrangements.

As I could only "meet" the golu dolls once a year, I'd eagerly wait for the crate to be unpacked, as if it were a box of birthday presents. My mom would buy a new doll every year to add to our collection. We would arrange the clay, wood, and porcelain dolls, as well as wax fruits and vegetables, on "grass" grown from mustard seeds to create miniature zoos and parks.

Golu dolls are passed down from one generation to the next. I have my great-grandmother's porcelain British orchestra from the colonial era!

I'd especially look forward to golu hopping, which is when we'd meet relatives I hadn't seen all year and visit friends and neighbors. This part of the Navarathri festivities renewed friendships and helped make new ones. The rituals were fun and made me feel special. Different, yummy sundal (legume snacks) every evening and gifts from every house we visited were fun bonuses!

Like Navya, Navarathri helped me find my Shakti to face my fears. I hope you find your Shakti too!

# Navya Sings for Navarathri

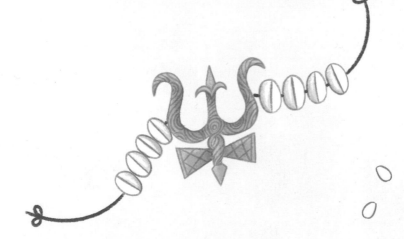

Words by Lakshmi Thamizhmani   Pictures by Avani Dwivedi

HARPER
*An Imprint of HarperCollinsPublishers*

It was the evening before the nine-night festival of Navarathri, and Navya's aunt and cousin had finally arrived all the way from India.

"Athai! Shruti!" Navya jumped up and down. "I'm so happy we get to celebrate together this year!"

The next morning, Amma practiced singing with Athai and Shruti for the festival concert that would take place on the ninth night. Navya clapped her cymbals, melting into Athai's melodies as her aunt's voice flitted from one note to the next, but Navya didn't sing.

"At the concert, you should sing the song I taught you last month," Athai said to Navya. "You'll sound great."

*Singing onstage?*

*In front of everyone?*

Just the thought churned a storm of fear in Navya's stomach.

"Ummm." Navya hesitated.

"It'll be fun." Shruti smiled.

"I don't know when I can visit again," Navya's aunt said. "I'd love it if you could join."

Navya wanted to say yes.

For Athai.

Instead, her fear spoke for her. "I'll sing next time."

Every evening of Navarathri, Navya visited friends.
Whenever she wanted to join the singing to praise the
goddesses, fear chased her voice away like a fierce bull.

At night, Navya sang Athai's songs to herself.

On the fourth day of the festival, Athai narrated the Navarathri story to Navya and Shruti. "And that's how Goddess Durga defeated the evil demon, Mahisha."

"Wasn't she even a little bit scared?" Navya asked. Athai smiled. "She's Shakti, a superwoman." *I wish I could be Shakti.*

After morning prayers the next day, Athai sniffled
and sneezed.
That evening she woke up with a terrible cold.
"Achoo! I'm afraid I can't perform."
A thought strummed in Navya's head all night long.
*I want to sing.*
*For Athai.*

Imagining herself on a stage filled Navya
with lots of fear, but a bit of excitement too.
*If I practice a lot, I won't be scared.*

On the sixth day, Navya swallowed her fear and asked, "Amma, can I sing in Athai's place?"

"Yes, it would mean a lot to her," Amma said.

"I'll help you!" Shruti chimed in.

Navya took a deep breath,
closed her eyes, and sang.
   Her voice trembled, but she didn't stop.
   "Nice! The words and beats are correct.
But Dha should sound one note higher than Pa.
Sa is the highest note," Shruti said.
   Encouraged, Navya tried again.
   "You're doing great," Shruti cheered.
"Let's continue after prayers."

Navya offered lentil fritters to the gods.
Tiny glass bulbs lit the golu steps, like a path to heaven.
The steps sparked an idea.
*A note for a step, each higher than the previous one.*
*When I scale the highest note, I can reach Durga!*

On the seventh night, Navya practiced to the tempo of raindrops drumming on the roof, starting slow, then picking up speed, like her song.

She concentrated, making sure her notes jumped up and down, landing steadily on the right steps.

*Sa Ma Ga Ma Dha Ni Sa!*

*Sa Ni Dha Ma Ga Ri Sa!*

*Brihadambikayai Namaste Namaste!*

Ma

Ga

Ma

Sa

On the ninth day, the fragrance of frangipani flowers woke Navya.
A familiar fear bellowed inside her.
*What if I mess up?*

At Shanti Aunty's for the ritual and feast honoring young girls,
Navya sat on a decorated chair.

Shanti Aunty colored her feet, dotted her
forehead with vermilion, and dressed her
hair with flowers. She also gifted Navya
a coral necklace.

Navya squirmed from the attention.

"The feast is for you. Today, *you* are worshipped as Shakti," Shanti Aunty said.

*I am Shakti?*

Chanting verses, Shanti Aunty touched Navya's feet, seeking blessings.

Navya felt magical.

On the way home, Navya sang.
Over and over.
In her head, to a crowd.
Out loud, to Shruti and Amma.
*I can do it!*

At dusk, guests gathered.
Amma sang first.
Shruti followed.
But Navya couldn't find her voice.
Her heart pounded like a drum.
She reached for Shruti and
cleared her throat. Hesitantly,
Navya started to sing.

Ma . . .

Ma  Ga

Sa

As Navya sang, she looked out at the crowd.
Fear crept back up, knocking her notes off-key.
She stopped singing, looking away.

There, glowing in the light of the silver lamps, the Durga doll
seemed to smile at her and say, *You'll sound great.*
Navya clutched her necklace, grabbing fear by its horns.
*I am Shakti!*

She took a deep breath, closed her eyes, and sang.

Her voice bloomed like a lotus.
Her notes soared like a swan.
Her spirit roared like a lion.
Navya sang free.

"You rocked!" Shruti said, grinning.
Athai hugged Navya. "You made me proud!"
"I knew you could!" Amma kissed her.
"I am Shakti!" Navya cheered. "When can I sing next?"

# ABOUT THE FESTIVAL

$\mathcal{N}$avarathri, literally meaning nine nights, is a Hindu festival celebrating feminine power in the Tamil month of Purattasi and the Sanskrit month of Ashwin, which fall in autumn around September or October.

All over India, goddesses Durga, Lakshmi, and Saraswathi are worshipped for three days each during the festival. Durga is the goddess of bravery and strength, Lakshmi is the goddess of prosperity and fortune, and Saraswathi is the goddess of learning and wisdom. Together they form a triad of power, wealth, and knowledge. Women use this festival as an opportunity to showcase their strengths, renew bonds, and worship each other as living goddesses.

The practice of keeping Kolu or Golu is prevalent in South India. This display of dolls of deities, ancient sages, national heroes, figurines representing urban and rural life, and toys of plants, animals, and birds is arranged from top to bottom on odd-numbered steps. Kids participate by adding their toys to the display. In some regions of India, each day of the festival is marked by its color, food, fruit, flower, leaf, decorative pattern, and musical raga. Every morning and evening, food offerings are made to the deities. Friends and families visit, sing prayers, eat snacks, and renew the social contract of goodwill and support. Some people perform special rituals—or pujas—to worship young girls as forms of Goddess Durga, which shows them their importance in society.

The ninth day of Navarathri is celebrated as Saraswathi Puja. Books and musical instruments are worshipped by applying sandalwood paste and vermilion kunkuma on them. It is believed that with Saraswathi's blessings, all endeavors undertaken the following day will be successful. Vijayadasami, the tenth day of the festival, is considered the day of victory and is a special day for children to start learning the alphabet, a new lesson, or a new craft. Even tools, cars, machines, and appliances are worshipped on this day. On the night of Vijayadasami, a special Aarati—a light offering to the gods as part of prayer—is performed to see the goddess off and one of the dolls is laid down on the step. The next day, they are packed away until the next Navarathri.

The festival is observed in many different ways all over India. In North India, devotees fast and enact the victory of King Rama over the demon Ravana. In East India, big Durga statues are set up on stages to honor the goddess's victory over the demon Mahisha, and on the tenth day, the statues are immersed in a body of water. In West India, special dances are performed on the nine nights, when devotees dance in circles around a Durga idol. Everywhere, the underlying theme of Navarathri is the victory of good over evil and the celebration of girlhood and womanhood.

## THE MYTH

*M*ahisha (also known as Mahishasura), the buffalo demon, prayed to Brahma, the Hindu God of creation, for many, many years. Pleased by his prayers, Brahma blessed Mahisha with his wish—that no one except a woman could defeat him. Mahisha was pretty sure that no woman would be strong enough to fight him (if you guessed he was wrong, you are right!).

Soon, Mahisha and his army wreaked havoc on Earth, and the gods fled in fear.

But the gods knew what to do. They combined their powers to create Goddess Durga, a super-powerful woman, and gave her their special weapons.

Durga fought Mahisha for nine days. The demon kept shape-shifting, trying to trick her. Finally, on the tenth day, Durga defeated him and restored peace.

Go, girl power!

# THE MUSIC

Carnatic music is a traditional vocal art form from Southern India.

Similar to the Western do-re-mi-fa-sol-la-ti / C-D-E-F-G-A-B, it has seven musical notes—sa-ri-ga-ma-pa-dha-ni—called swarams, that can be combined in different ways and scales to form melody patterns called ragams. There are seventy-two fundamental ragams and thousands of derived ragams. Carnatic music consists of ragam-based compositions that are sung by musicians and played on instruments. Cyclical rhythmic beats made by hand and finger movements, called thalams, determine the pace at which songs are sung, while sruthi notes determine the pitch interval.

Today, Carnatic music festivals are conducted around the world, notably in the cities of Thiruvayaru and Chennai in India and Cleveland, Ohio, in the United States.

# GLOSSARY

**amma (UM-mah):** mom

**athai (AH-tay):** paternal aunt

**golu (GOH-loo):** also known as kolu, an arrangement of small dolls on an odd number of wooden steps during the Navarathri festival

**Navarathri (nah-vah-RAH-three):** nine-night Hindu festival celebrating the victory of good over evil

**Shakti (SHAK-tee):** divine female power

**Durga (DUR-ga):** Goddess symbolizing strength, created by the gods to fight the evil Mahisha

**Mahisha (muh-he-shah):** A shape-shifting buffalo demon who fought the gods; a symbol of ignorance

# PROTEIN-PACKED NAVRATHRI
# CHICKPEA SNACK RECIPE

*T*he vadai fritters shown in the story are made in the morning, while this chickpea snack is made in the evening. A popular yet simple dish, this sundal snack is made in most South Indian Tamil households during Navarathri and other festivals. I'd gobble bowlfuls at home and am always hungry for more when golu hopping.

   You will need an adult's help to make this delicious dish.

Vegan, gluten-free, soy-free

Preparation and cooking time: 20 minutes

Servings: 2

## Ingredients

2 teaspoons coconut oil* (or any cooking oil)

¼ teaspoon mustard seeds*

¾ teaspoon urad dal (skinned black gram)*

½ sprig (about 6) curry leaves*

¼ teaspoon salt

¼ teaspoon turmeric powder*

Pinch of gluten-free hing (asafoetida)*

½ green Thai chili (optional, if you like it spicy)

One 14-oz can unsalted garbanzo beans (chickpeas), drained and rinsed

1 tablespoon fresh or thawed, grated, unsweetened coconut*

*You can find these ingredients in any Indian grocery store.

## Instructions

Step 1: Heat the oil on medium-high. Once the oil is hot, add the mustard seeds.

Step 2: After the mustard seeds sputter, add the urad dal and roast until they turn a light golden color.

Step 3: Lower the heat to medium-low.

Step 4: Add the curry leaves, salt, turmeric, and hing. Toss and fry until the leaves turn crisp and dark green.

Step 5 (optional): If you like spicy sundal, add the chili and cook for one more minute.

Step 6: Add the garbanzo beans and toss for two minutes so they cook well in the spice mix.

Step 7: Turn off the heat. Mix in the grated coconut, and let it sit for two minutes.

Tip:
Adding more coconut will increase the flavor.

For my Shaktis—
Shivaani and Mishika—L. T.

For Shadra
and all the women who inspire and encourage me.—A. D.

Library of Congress Control Number: 2023944534
ISBN 978-0-06-328603-0

The artist used watercolor, gouache, ink and pencil colors
to create the illustrations for this book.
Typography by Caitlin E. D. Stamper
24 25 26 27 28 RTLO 10 9 8 7 6 5 4 3 2 1
First Edition